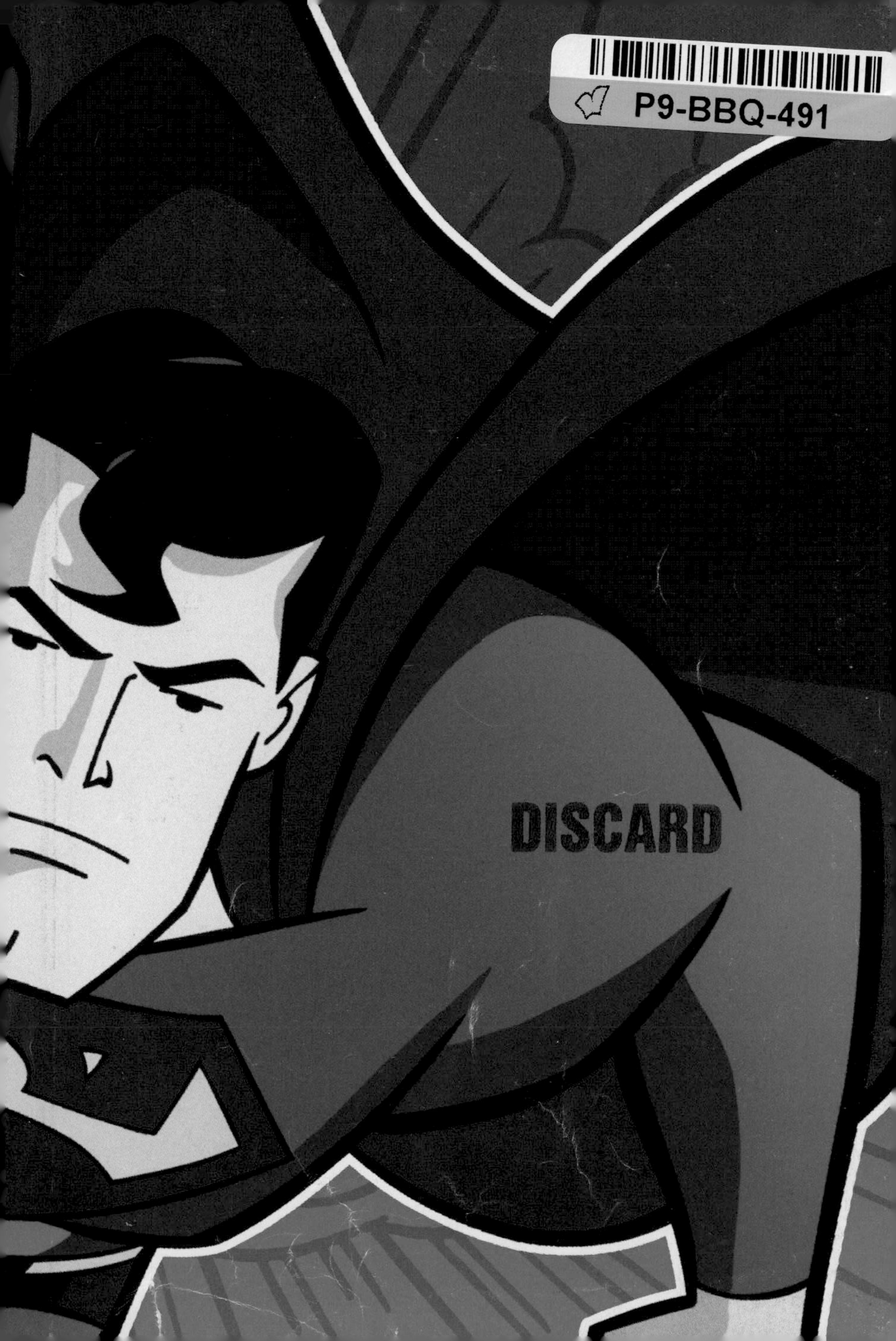

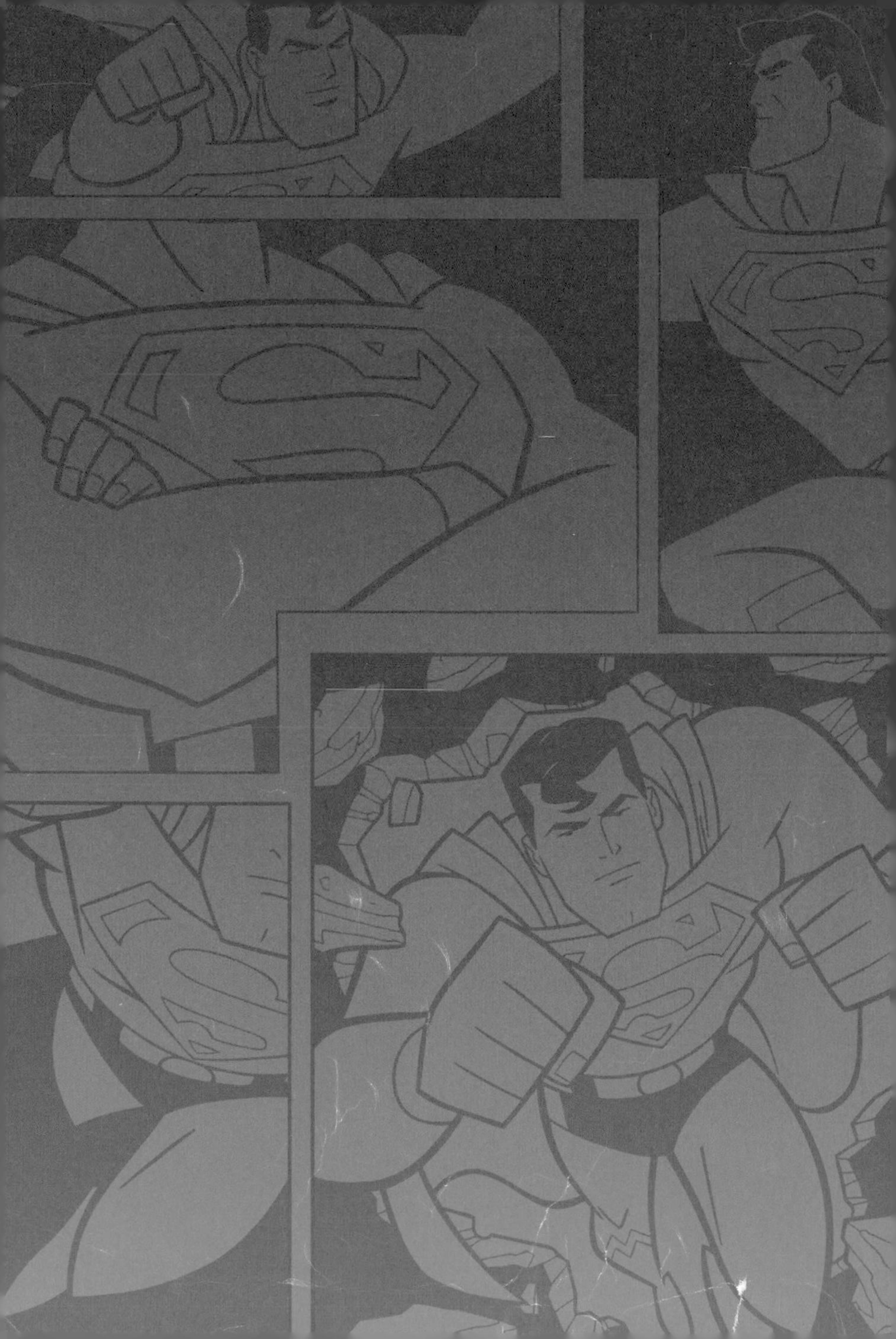

SUPER DC HEROES

SUPERMAN

COSMIC BOUNTY HUNTER

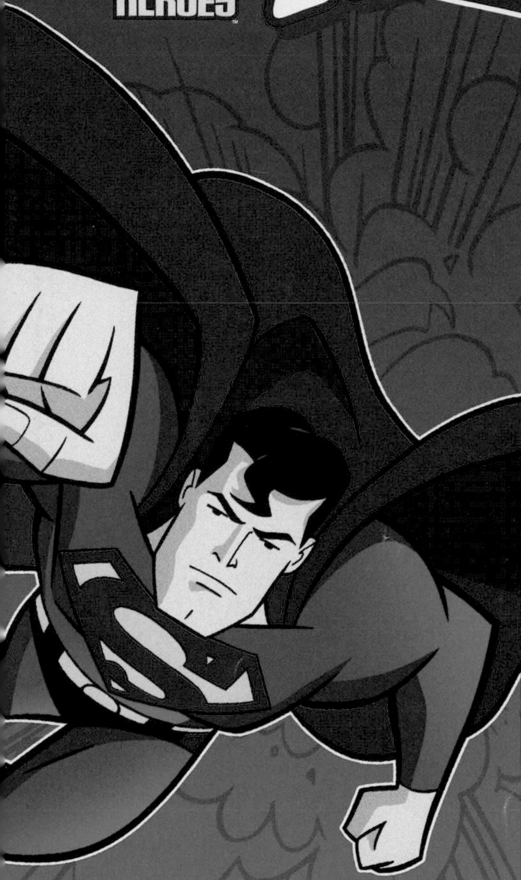

WRITTEN BY
BLAKE A. HOENA

ILLUSTRATED BY
RICK BURCHETT AND
LEE LOUGHRIDGE

SUPERMAN CREATED BY
JERRY SIEGEL AND
JOE SHUSTER

LOBO CREATED BY
ROGER SLIFER AND
KEITH GIFFEN

STONE ARCH BOOKS
a capstone imprint

Published by Stone Arch Books in 2011
A Capstone Imprint
151 Good Counsel Drive, P.O. Box 669
Mankato, Minnesota 56002
www.capstonepub.com

Cataloging-in-Publication Data is available on the Library of Congress
website.

ISBN: 978-1-4342-2133-9 (library binding)
ISBN: 978-1-4342-2769-0 (paperback)

Summary: Intergalactic bounty hunter Lobo has a new job. The evil aliens
Kalibak and Desaad have hired him to capture Superman, dead or alive!
However, when Lobo finally manages to wrangle up the Man of Steel, the
aliens aren't far behind. They don't trust the ill-mannered bounty hunter,
and quickly trap him beneath a force field with Superman. Lobo and the
Man of Steel must set aside their differences in order to escape, capture the
two villains, and collect the well-deserved reward.

Art Director: Bob Lentz
Designer: Hilary Wacholz
Production Specialist: Michelle Biedscheid

Printed in the United States of America in Stevens Point, Wisconsin.
032010
005741WZF10

TABLE OF CONTENTS

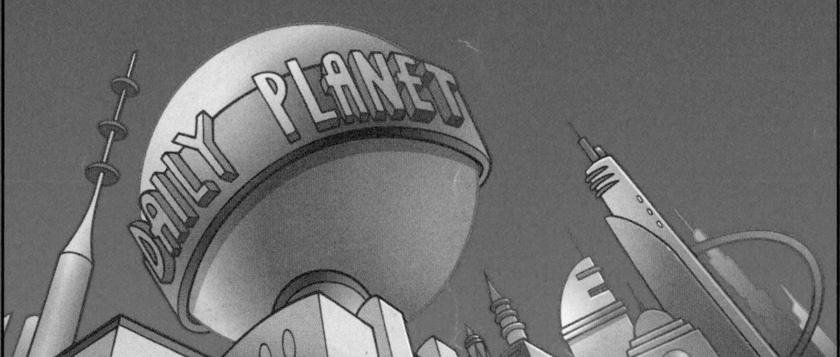

DAILY PLANET

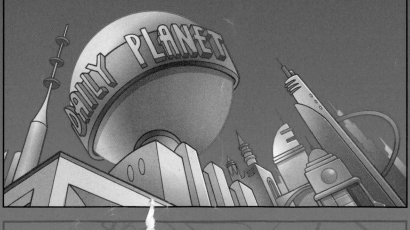

CHAPTER 1

THE BOUNTY HUNTER

On the faraway planet of Apokolips, a spaceship rumbled to a halt, kicking up a cloud of dirt and debris on the landing pad. When the dust cleared, a door in the ship's side slid open. Out stepped Lobo, the universe's most ruthless bounty hunter. He was tall and muscular. He wore biker boots and a black leather jacket. Over one shoulder, he cradled a crowbar.

Behind Lobo, a troop of Apokolips soldiers stumbled out of the spaceship. Some of them wore bandages around their heads. Others had arms in slings.

Next to the landing pad was a walkway. It led toward a menacing looking castle off in the distance. Lobo's lengthy strides quickly carried him toward the castle's front door. The alien soldiers followed.

With a swing of his crowbar, Lobo bashed the door down. **KRAK!** He then kicked through its splintered remains and headed down a wide hallway.

THUD! THUD! His boots stomped loudly on the stone floor. The soldiers trembled behind him.

At the end of the hallway, large brass doors swung inward, revealing the castle's throne room.

"Come in," a deep voice boomed from within.

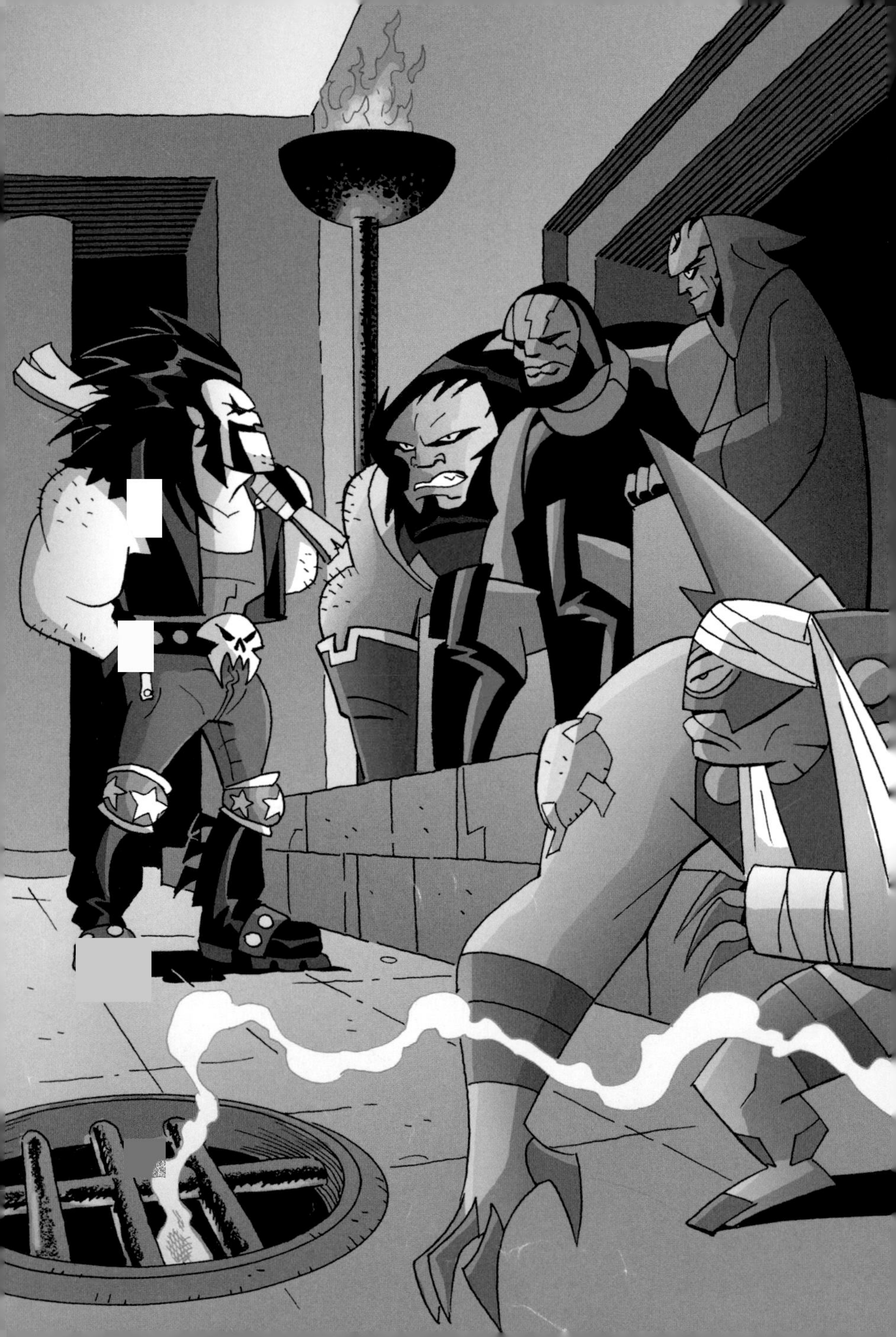

Lobo advanced, and the Apokolips soldiers poured into the room after him.

On the opposite side of the throne room sat Darkseid, ruler of Apokolips. To his right stood his son, the ogre-like Kalibak. On his left was the evil scientist Desaad.

"Thank you for coming," Darkseid said to Lobo. "I hope my minions didn't bother you."

The soldiers now formed a half circle around Lobo.

"They *did* interrupt my nap," Lobo snarled. "So I had to break of a few of them."

Several of the bandaged aliens shuddered as Lobo shifted his crowbar from one shoulder to the other.

"I wouldn't have asked you here if it wasn't important," Darkseid said.

"What could be more important than my beauty sleep?" Lobo said, standing proudly in front of Apokolips' ruler. "It's not easy looking this good."

Darkseid stood up and walked over to Lobo, placing a hand on the bounty hunter's shoulder. "Have you heard of Superman?" he asked.

"Yeah, we've tangled a time or two," Lobo replied. "What do you want with him?"

"Come this way," Darkseid said.

He led Lobo behind his throne. "Superman's been quite bothersome," Darkseid explained. "He's always in the way of my plans to conquer Earth."

"And I need something to be done about that," Darkseid continued.

"What do you expect little ol' me to do to Superman?" Lobo asked.

The pair stopped walking. They now stood behind the throne.

"Your job," Darkseid said. "You're a bounty hunter after all."

"Hey, even though he wears tights and a cape, Superman's no pushover," Lobo said. "It's gonna cost you so some serious cha-ching if you're asking me to take him on, buddy."

"Will this be enough to hire your services?" Darkseid asked, motioning to the wall next to them. **CLANK! CHING!** A door burst open, and a pile of jewels, gems, and trinkets spilled onto the floor.

Lobo rushed over to the loot. Kneeling down on the floor, he grabbed two fists full of treasure and raised them above his head.

"Man, with this, I could buy new chrome headers for my bike!" Lobo exclaimed. "And I'd still have enough for that beach house near Alpha Centauri. I could probably even get front-row seats at next year's asteroid smash-up derby or . . ."

While Lobo dreamed of what he would do with his reward, Desaad walked up to Darkseid and placed a long, cylindrical object in his hand. Raising the object above his head, Darkseid flipped a switch. **CLICK!** The object emitted a chain of crackling and sizzling energy. With of flick of his wrist, Darkseid snapped the chain toward Lobo. It wrapped around the bounty hunter, trapping him.

"Owwww!" Lobo shouted. "What gives?"

"It's a gift," Darkseid explained. "It was designed by my scientist, Desaad. It will help you capture Superman."

CLICK! Darkseid flicked the switch off, and the chain of energy disappeared. He then flipped the weapon to Lobo, who caught it with an outstretched hand.

"Cool! It's like my birthday, only better," Lobo chuckled. "I don't have to blow out some stupid candles to get my wish — a chance to put the smackdown on a super do-gooder."

"Do you need help reaching Earth?" Darkseid asked.

"Nah, I got my own ride," Lobo replied.

Lobo whistled loudly. In the distance, a thunderous roar was heard. A motorcycle rumbled into the throne room, scattering the soldiers in its path. Lobo hopped on and revved its engine.

VROOOOOM! VROOOOOM!

"Next time I see you, you'll have a date with Superman," Lobo shouted as he roared off.

After the bounty hunter left, Desaad and Kalibak walked up to Darkseid. "I don't like him," Kalibak said with a grumble.

"He doesn't seem trustworthy," added Desaad.

"All that matters," Darkseid began, "is that Lobo weakens Superman enough for our plan to work."

The three of them smiled wickedly.

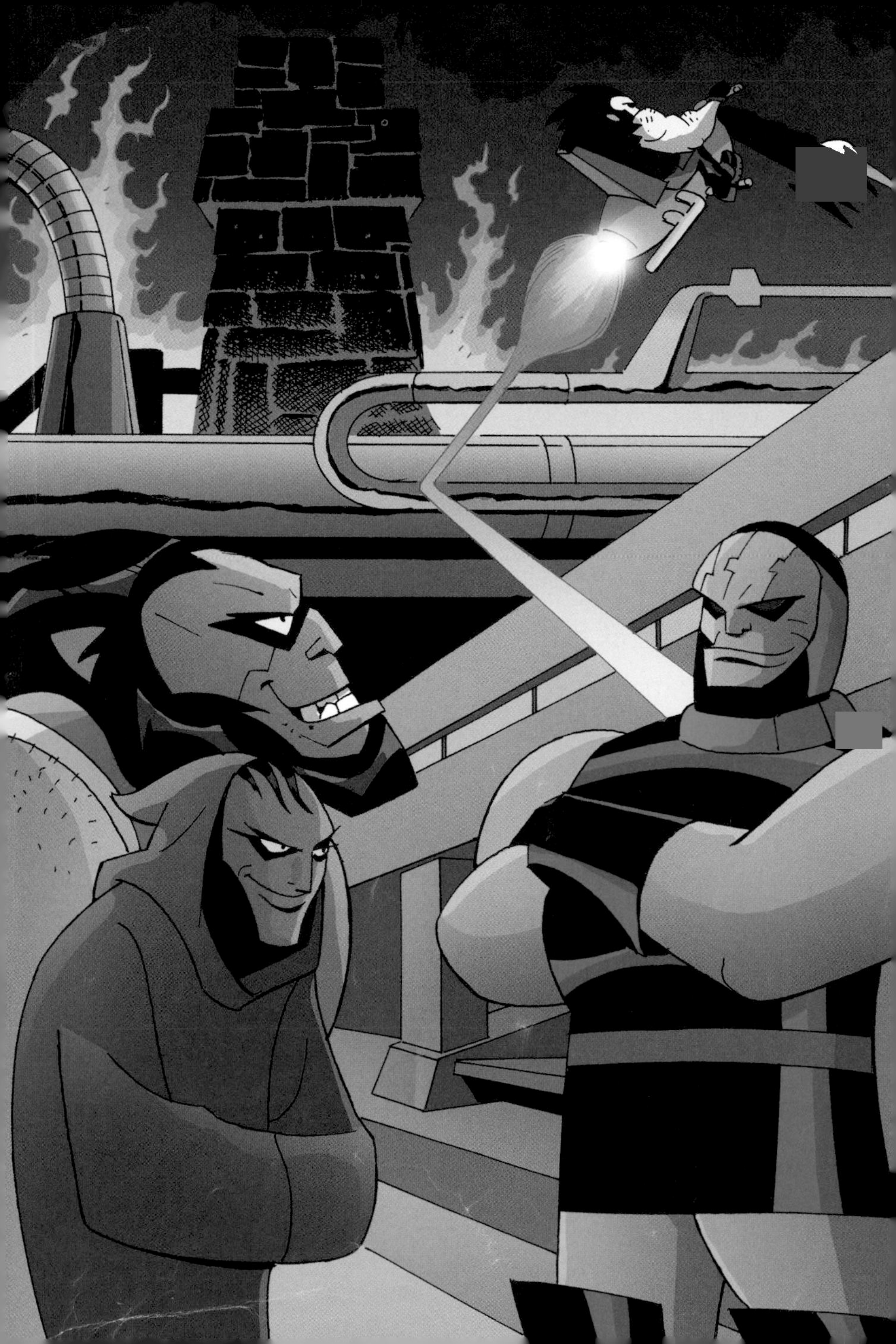

CHAPTER 2

TO THE RESCUE!

In the newsroom of the Daily Planet Building, Lois Lane stormed over to the desk of fellow reporter Clark Kent.

"Clark," she said, waving a copy of the *Daily Planet* newspaper in front Clark's face. "How is it that some country bumpkin from Smallville can beat me to one of Metropolis' juiciest stories?"

On the front page of the newspaper, the headline read "Superman Saves Shock Jock Leslie Willis, by Clark Kent."

"Lucky, I guess," Clark replied with a smile.

FLAP! Lois tossed the paper down on Clark's desk. "Luck!" Lois shouted. "I was reporting the news in this city while you were still out milking cows, and that's your explanation?!"

"Maybe I just have a heightened sense for news," Clark added.

"Ooooh," Lois fumed, and then stomped off.

Out of the corner of his eye, Clark saw Jimmy Olsen, a young staff photographer. He was chuckling about the exchange between Lois and Clark.

"Better not get on her bad side today, Jimmy," Clark warned, "or she'll drag you all around town looking for a story."

"I know. I know," Jimmy said. "It's just funny seeing how upset she gets when she doesn't get the front page story."

Jimmy glanced down. "So, what are you working on, Clark?" he asked.

"An interview I did with Superman," replied Clark.

"Cool, can I read it when you're done?" questioned Jimmy.

"Sure," Clark said. He turned back to his work, typing up the story on Superman.

Unknown to Lois and Jimmy, Clark had a secret identity. He was Superman, Last Son of Krypton. The rays from Earth's yellow sun gave him superpowers, such as superhuman strength, the ability to fly, and super-hearing.

A short time later, Clark stopped typing.

Clark tilted his head to one side. Over the clicks of his keyboard, he thought he had heard a cry for help. He waited.

"HELP!" There it was again, off in the distance. Clark leaped from his desk and headed for the exit.

"Hey, where are you going?" Lois yelled after him. "You better not be chasing some new story."

"No, no," Clark yelled, darting out the door. "I spilled coffee on my shirt and need to go home to get a change of clothes."

Once outside, Clark quickly ducked into a deserted alley. Making sure no one was watching him, he shed his shirt and tie, revealing a blue uniform with a red "S" emblazoned on the chest. Superman then leaped into the air and flew away.

In the distance, he saw a bridge swaying back and forth. Cars and trucks skidded across the pavement and crashed into the guardrails. The people inside the vehicles screamed in fright. Then one car flipped off the bridge, falling toward the river far below.

Superman quickly swooped down under the car, catching the vehicle before it splashed into the water.

As he placed the car safely on the shore, Superman looked up at the teetering bridge. Any minute, another car could come tumbling from its heights. He couldn't stop them all.

"I knew it," a voice chuckled behind Superman. "All I needed to do was cause a little trouble, and you'd show up."

Superman whirled around. The alien bounty hunter Lobo leaned against one of the bridge's supports.

"Lobo!" Superman exclaimed. "What are you doing here?"

"You don't seem happy to see me!" Lobo said.

"Not when you're putting people in harm's way," Superman scolded.

CRAAAAACK!! Lobo punched the bridge support. Distant screams were heard as the bridge shook.

CRUNCH! CRASH!!

A few large bricks crashed to the ground between him and Superman. Lobo picked up one of the bricks, which was about the size of a TV, and tossed up it and down in the air.

"I knew if I threatened some of these puny earthlings," Lobo said, "you'd come running, all hero-like."

"Well, you found me," Superman said. "Now what do you want?"

Lobo caught the brick in his hand. He smiled wickedly, and his knuckles whitened. Then he laughed.

"This!" Lobo shouted.

Lobo threw the brick at Superman. It hit the Man of Steel in the chest and sent him reeling backward. **SLAM!** Lobo then grabbed a nearby car and lifted it over his head. **SMASH!** He slammed it down on Superman. The Man of Steel fell to the ground in a cloud of dust.

"Owwww," Lobo winced. "That's gotta hurt."

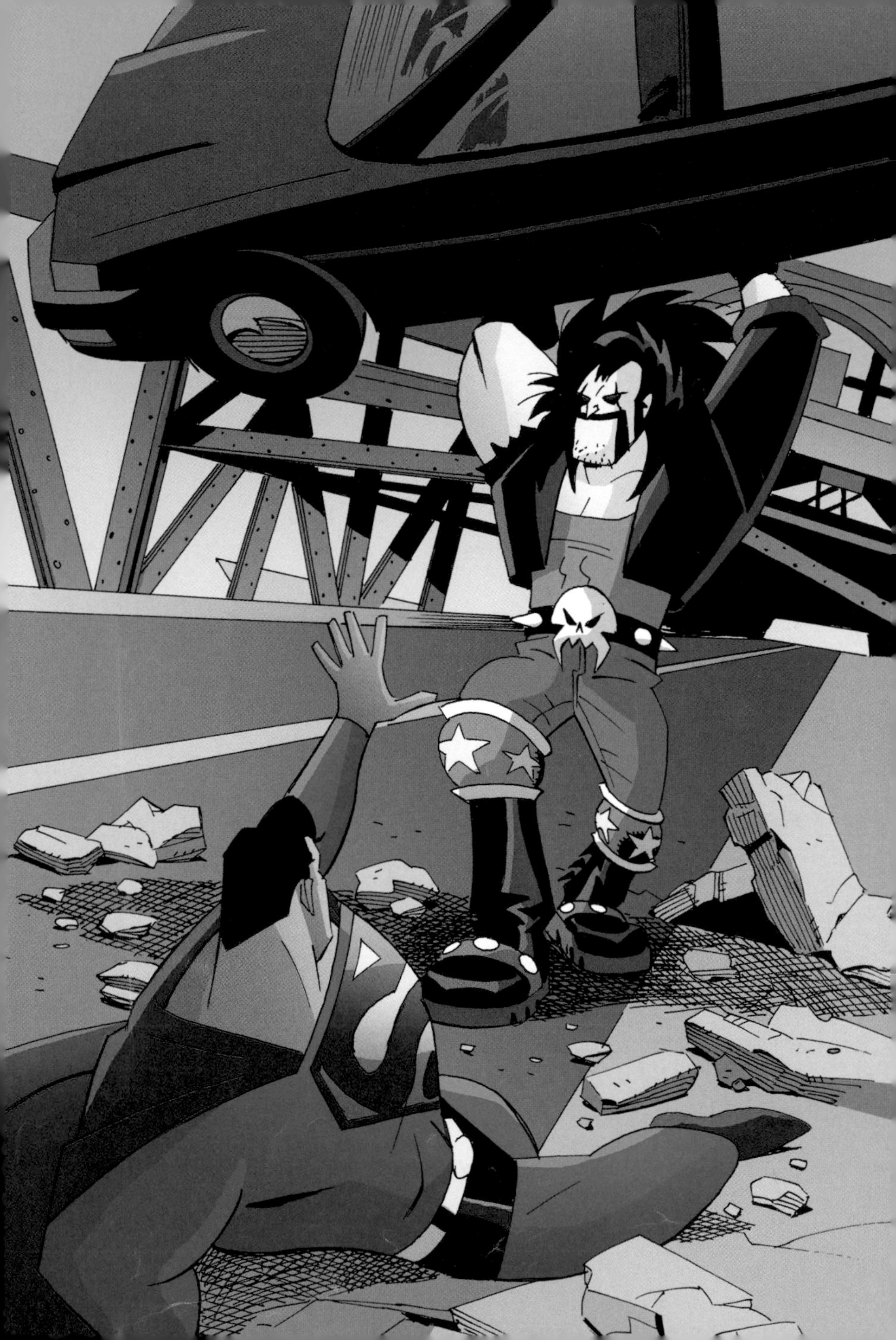

"But I have another surprise for you," Lobo added. Superman sat there completely stunned.

From his back pocket, Lobo whipped out the weapon that Darkseid had given him. He clicked the switch.  A chain of red energy, crackling and sizzling, dangled from it.

"What's that?" Superman asked, eyeing Lobo's weapon.

"Oh, just a little gift from a mutual friend," Lobo said. With a flick of wrist, Lobo sent the chain of energy whipping out at Superman.

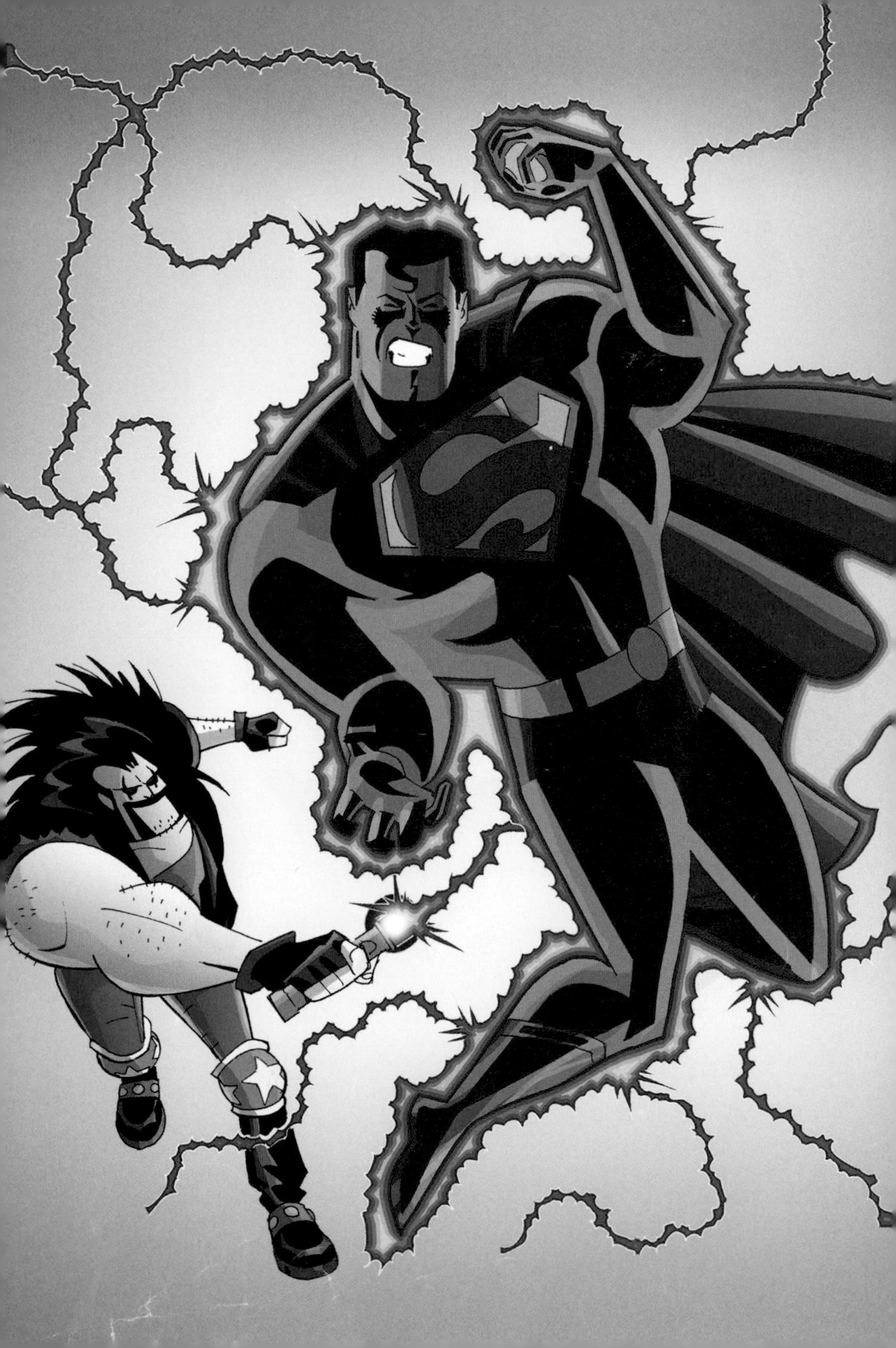

CHAPTER 3

ALIEN FACE-OFF

"Ahhh!" Superman moaned in pain.

Lobo released the chain of energy at Superman again. And for the second time, the powerful weapon struck the Man of Steel. **ZZZAPPPPPPP!**

"Argh!" Superman yelled.

"Tickles, doesn't it?" Lobo laughed.

"You think this is funny?" said Superman.

"Yeah, kinda," Lobo replied, smirking from ear to ear.

Lobo whipped the energy chain at Superman another time. This time, though, the Man of Steel was ready for the attack. He ducked under the sizzling energy blast, and then leaped at Lobo, slugging him in the stomach. **THUD!**

"Ummmpf!" Lobo grunted as he fell.

The pair rolled to the ground, fists flying and feet kicking. While Superman and Lobo fought, a car drove up and skidded to a stop near them. **SKREEE-EEE-EEECH!** Out jumped Lois and Jimmy Olsen.

"Quick, Jimmy," Lois shouted. "Snap a couple pictures of them fighting. This is definitely worth a front-page story!"

FLASH! FLASH! Jimmy started clicking away with his camera while Lois scribbled down notes.

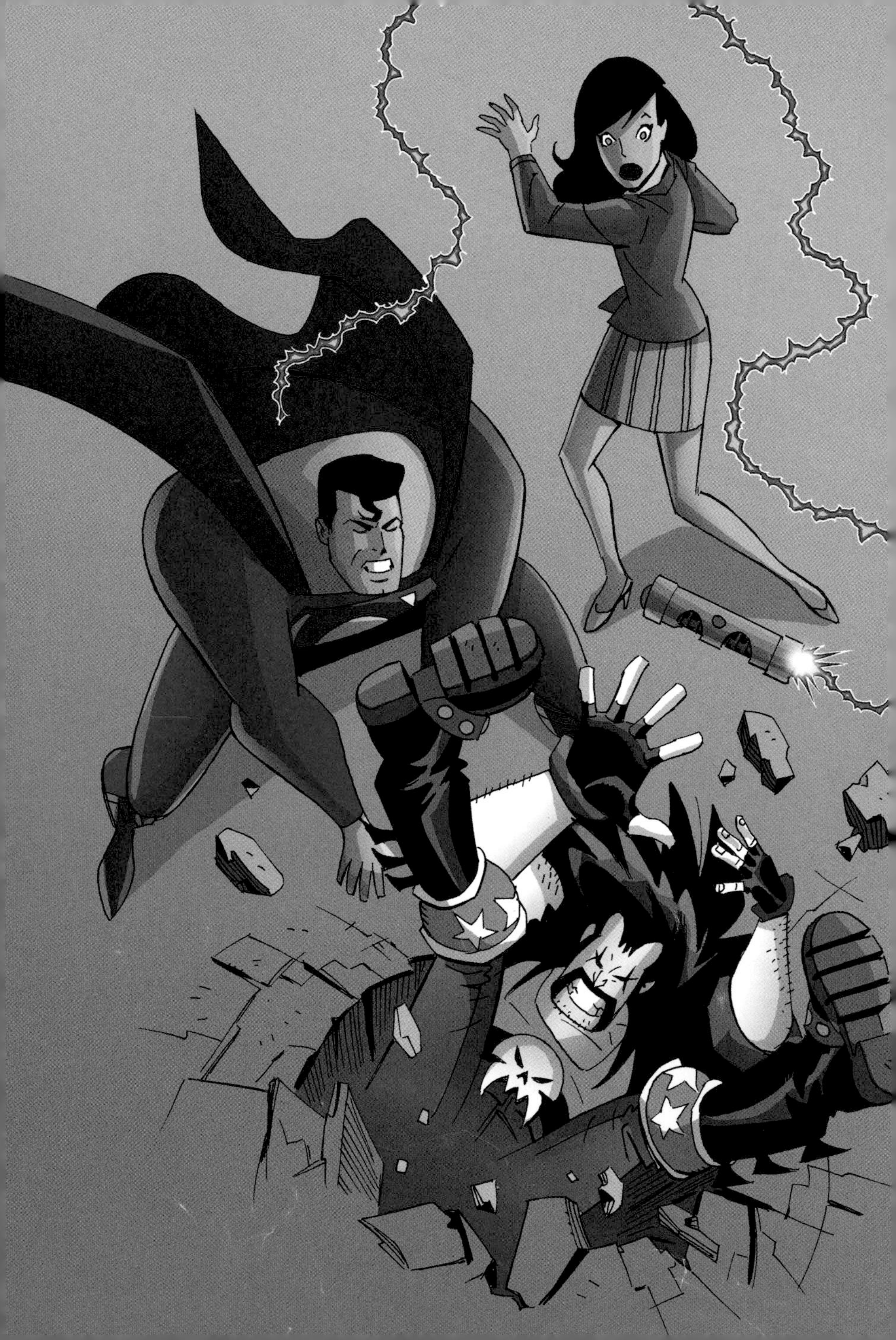

Suddenly, Superman slammed Lobo down on the ground with a thud, pinning him. Lobo's weapon flew out of his hand and high into the air. It landed at Lois' feet, with the chain of energy still dangling behind. **FZZT! FZZT!** Sparks were flying everywhere.

Lois reached down to pick up the weapon.

"Lois, be careful!" Superman shouted. He was worried she would get hurt.

While Superman was distracted, Lobo struck him square in the jaw. **POW!** The Man of Steel went sailing through the air and crashed to the ground. **THUD!**

Lobo then walked over to Lois. "I'll take that," he said. Lobo snatched the weapon from her.

Lobo spun around to face Superman, who was struggling to his feet.

"Fun time is over," Lobo snarled. "I have a job to do."

He raised the chain of energy above his head. It crackled. Then Lobo flicked the weapon at Superman, and the beam wrapped tightly around the Man of Steel.

Superman groaned and cried out in pain. He struggled with all his might to break free. Sparks shot out from the energy chain in all directions and seared everything they touched. Smoke filled the air. Then finally, after several minutes, Superman sank to his knees, exhausted.

"Ha!" Lobo laughed. "I didn't think Darkseid's toy would be able to hold you."

Just then, Lois ran over to Lobo. She repeatedly slammed her fists into his chest. "You let him go!" she yelled. "Let him go!"

Lobo reach down with his free hand and lifted Lois off the ground. She continued to try hitting and kicking him, and screamed loudly.

"Whoa, miss," Lobo laughed. "You seem to have quite the temper. Maybe you need to cool off in the river over there."

"But that's more than a hundred yards away!" Jimmy shouted.

"I bet you Superman's boots I can toss her that far," Lobo bragged.

"No, no!" Jimmy shouted.

Lobo wound up and gave a mighty heave. WHOOOOSH!

AAAAHHH! Lois screamed as she sailed through the air.

Superman stood up, looking angry.

"Uh-oh, did that make Mr. Goody Two-Shoes mad?" Lobo said, grinning.

Straining his muscles as hard as he could, Superman fought to break free of the chain of energy that was binding him. Lobo's weapon began to whir and spark. Then it burst into flames and blew up in Lobo's hand.

ZHHINNGG!!

"Ow!" Lobo exclaimed.

As Lobo was holding his sore hand, Superman was off in a flash, flying after Lois. He caught her just as she was about splash into the middle of the river.

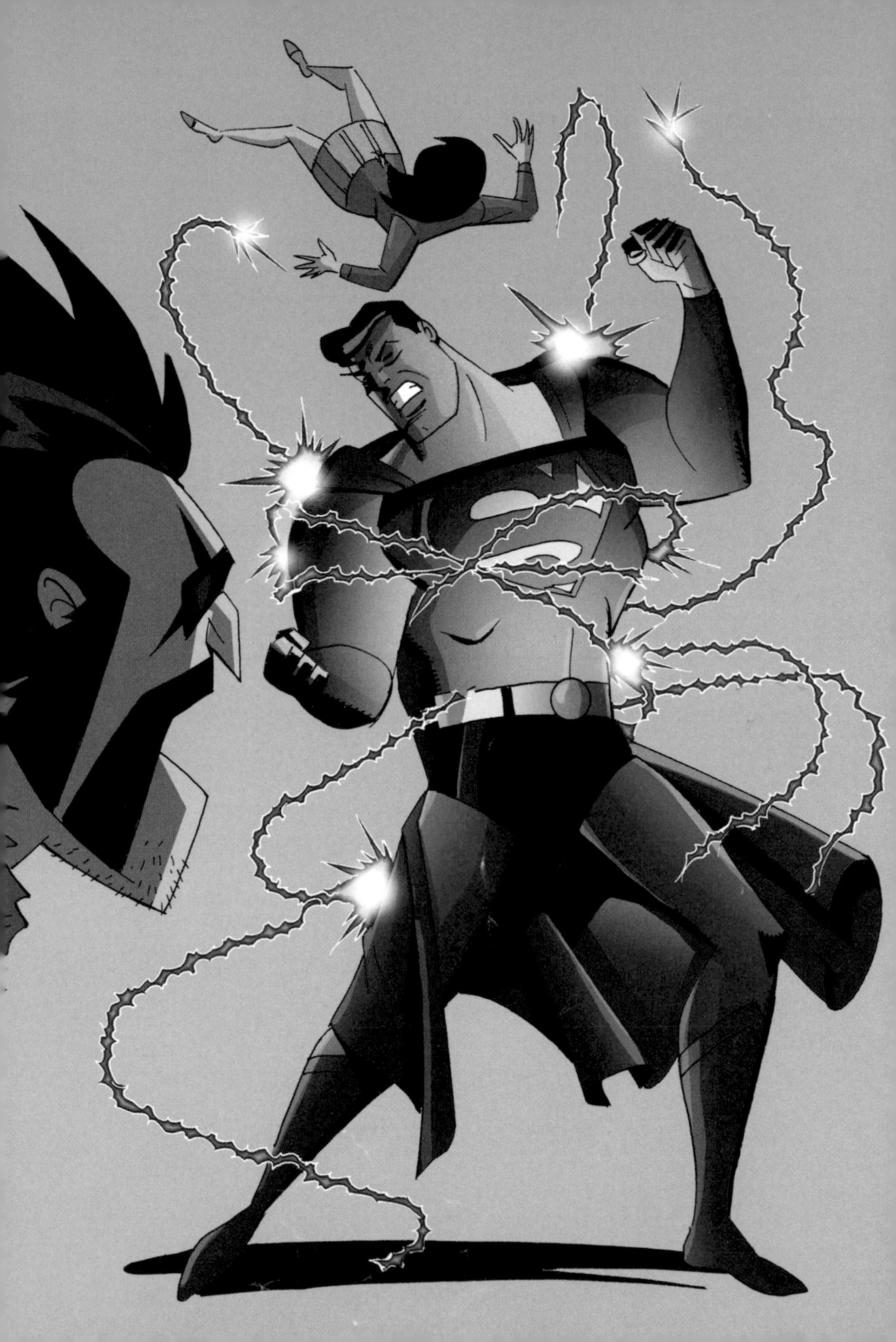

"Thanks, Superman," she said, hugging the Man of Steel.

"Now, it's time to stop Lobo," Superman said, setting Lois down on the bank of the river, "before someone gets hurt."

He was off again, zooming toward Lobo.

Superman crashed into the bounty hunter, and they rolled to the ground. After a couple brief moments, Superman stood victorious, holding Lobo over his head.

Suddenly, a blue energy field surrounded both super-strong fighters.

"Is this your doing?" Superman asked, dropping Lobo to the ground with a heavy thud.

"Nah," Lobo replied. "I don't like force fields. Body bags are more my style."

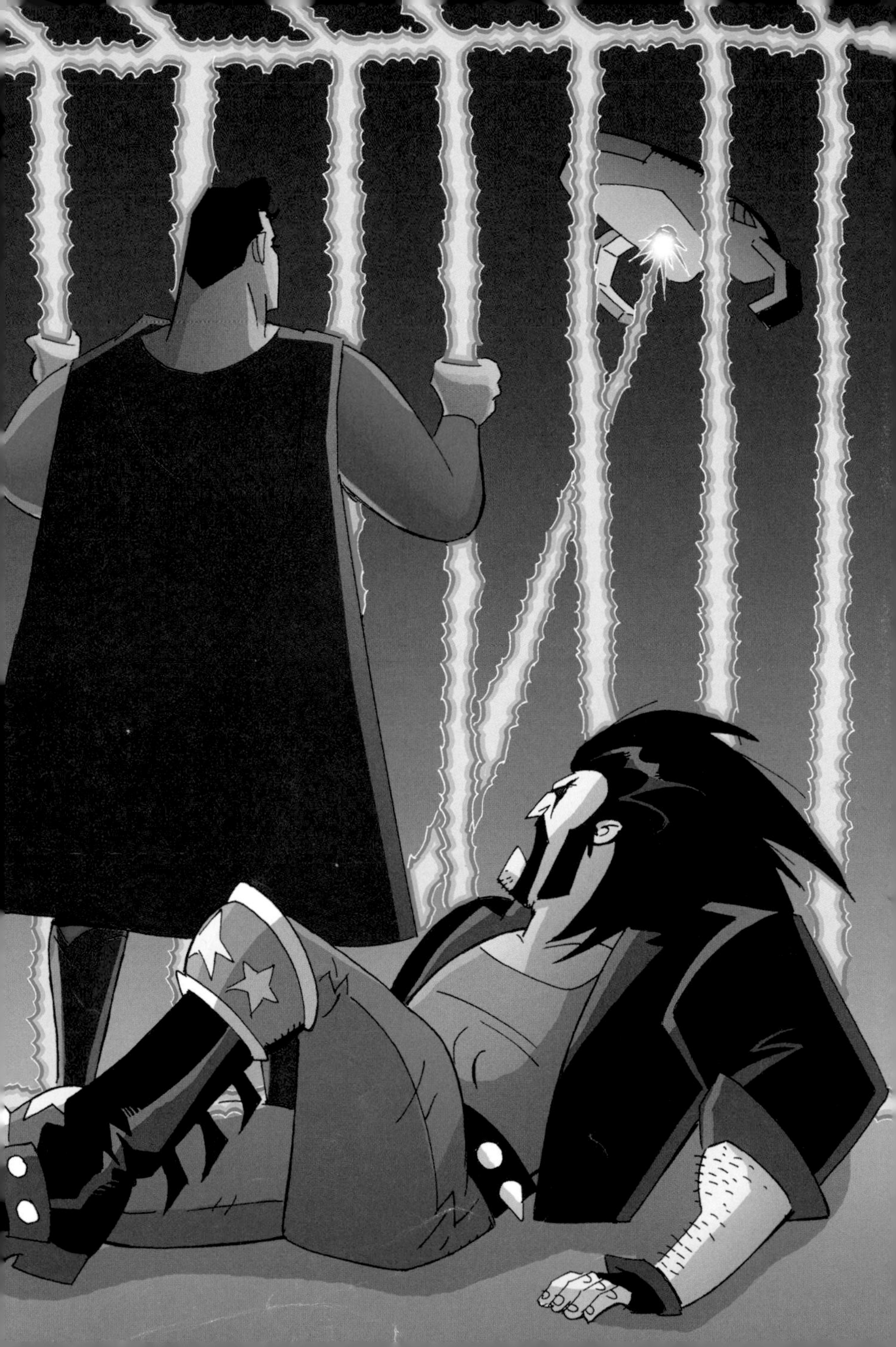

CHAPTER 4

KALIBAK AND DESAAD

As Superman looked upward, he saw a giant airship. The blue energy rays were coming from it.

"Darkseid . . ." Superman muttered.

As soon as a door in the ship's hull whooshed open, Kalibak and Desaad stepped out of the ship. Lobo began to yell at them. "Hey, what gives!" he shouted. "This wasn't part of our deal."

Lobo struck the force field. **ZZRRRRTT!** It didn't burst, just sizzled and flickered.

"I should have known you were behind Lobo's new toy, Desaad," Superman said.

"It seems you figured that out a little late, Superman," Desaad replied as he inspected the force field around Superman and Lobo.

Turning to Kalibak, he added, "The force field is secure. I guess now we'll have two new residents in the Apokolips dungeons instead of one."

"You dirty, rotten —" Lobo fumed. "When I get a hold of you . . ."

Kalibak and Desaad walked back to the ship, laughing.

Superman struck the force field as hard as he could. A loud SNAP! was heard as it flickered under the might of Superman's blow, but the force field didn't give.

The spaceship lifted off, floating above where Superman and Lobo where trapped. Then a large steel cable lowered down, and pulled the force field inside the ship. The hull doors closed. Now, they were surrounded by electronics, and all sorts of strange devices.

Superman leaned into the force field with all his strength. It snapped and fizzled, but it still didn't budge.

"Hey, Mr. Blue Tights," Lobo mocked Superman. "If I couldn't bust through that force field, little chance you have of doing it."

"Shhh," Superman said.

As he continued to push, Superman heard something. From the corner of the ship, he heard a high-pitched sound.

The harder he pushed, the louder it got.

Superman turned to Lobo. "Quick," he said. "What did they hire you to do?"

"To bring you back to Apokolips," Lobo replied.

"And that weapon?" Superman asked.

"I was told it would help capture you," Lobo said.

"See that box on the wall over there?" Superman said to Lobo. "That controls the force field."

"Yeah, so?" Lobo snorted.

"Desaad created this force field to capture me," Superman said. "They didn't plan on you being in here, too."

"At least that better have been their plan," Lobo said, growling.

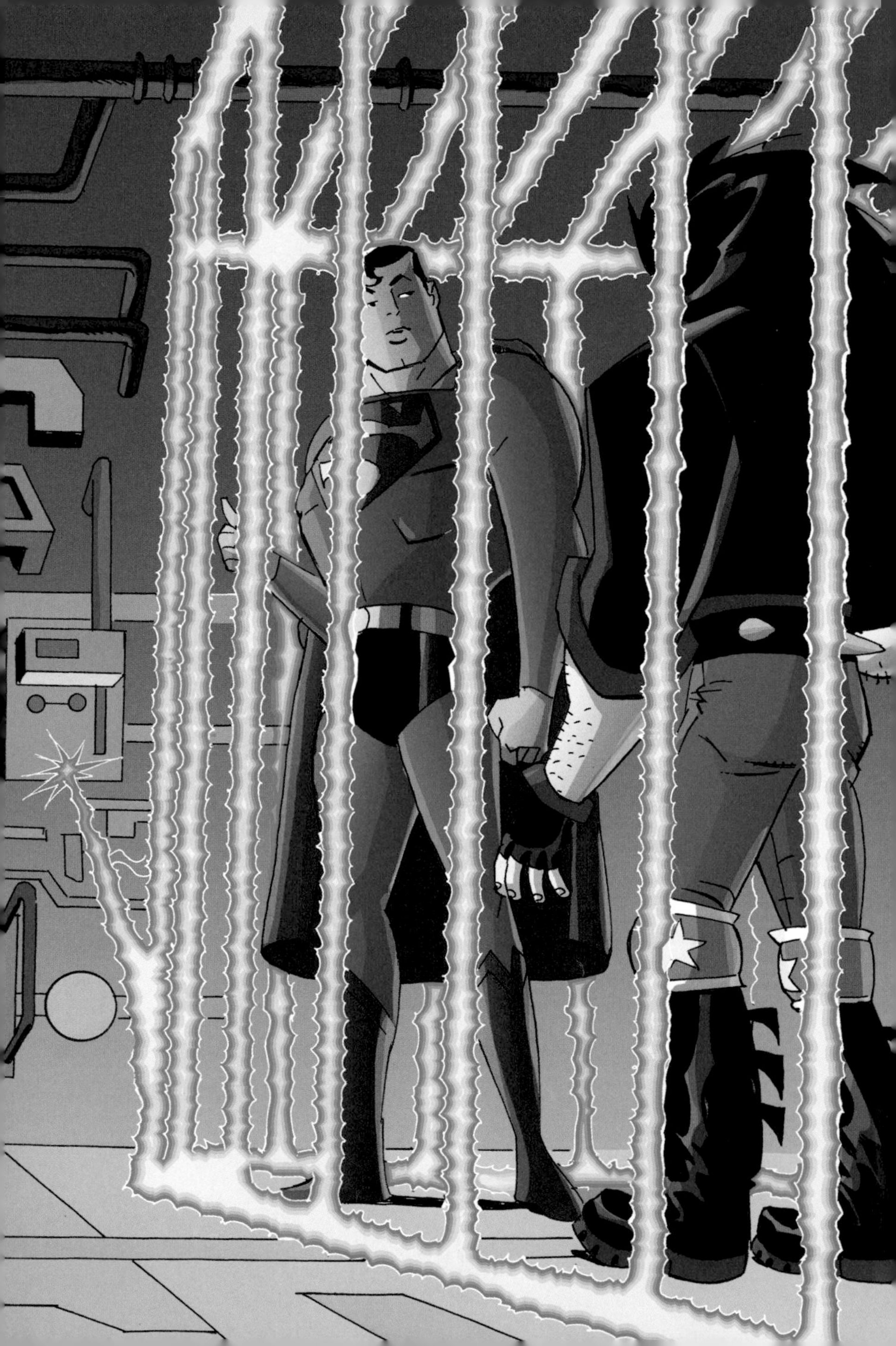

"Well maybe, if the two of us work together," Superman explained, "we can drain the controller of its power and break free."

As they were talking, the ship shot upward. It flew even higher into the sky.

"We'd better hurry," Superman yelled over the sound of the rushing wind. "Soon, they'll enter a boom tube, which will take us all to Apokolips. We may never escape."

"Hey, if this gives me a chance to knock Kalibak and Desaad's heads together," Lobo said, "then I'll give it a try."

Lobo pounded on the wall of the force field. It crackled under the pressure of his fist, but did not seem to weaken.

But Superman knew the high-pitched whining sound was getting louder.

Superman leaned into the wall of the force field, opposite of Lobo. He pushed with all his strength while Lobo smashed the force field with his fist. The controller began to squeal loudly and smoke.

"Just a little more," Superman shouted.

Suddenly, the controller exploded!

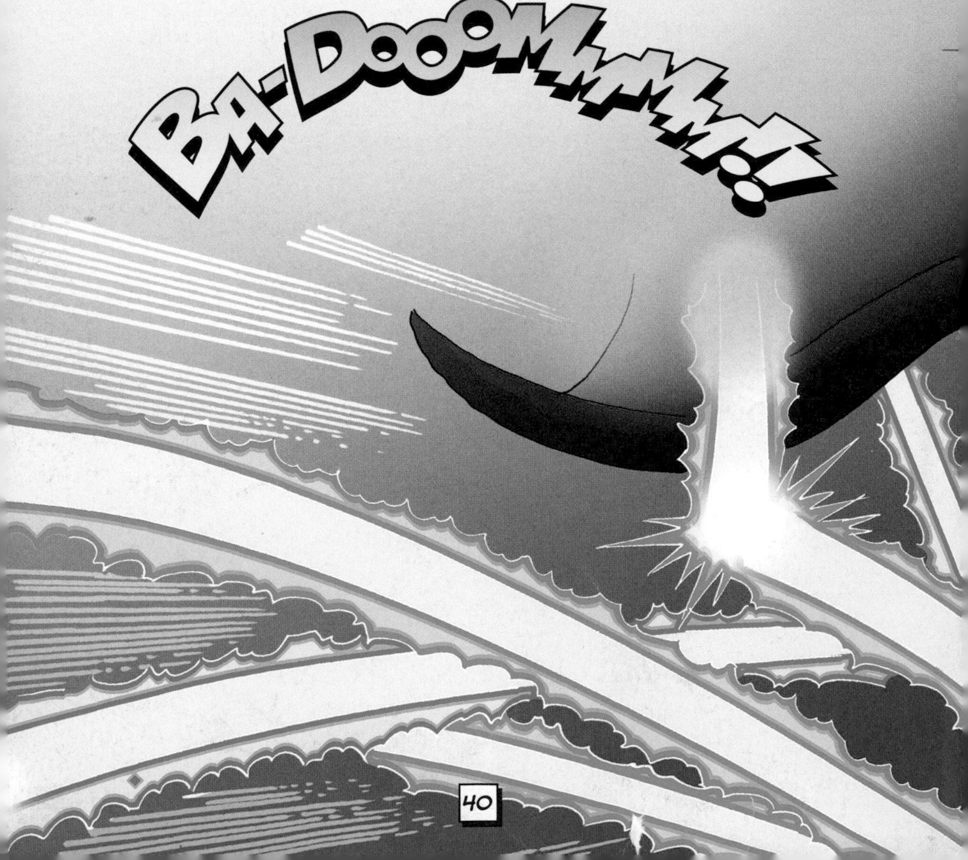
BA-DOOOMMMM!!

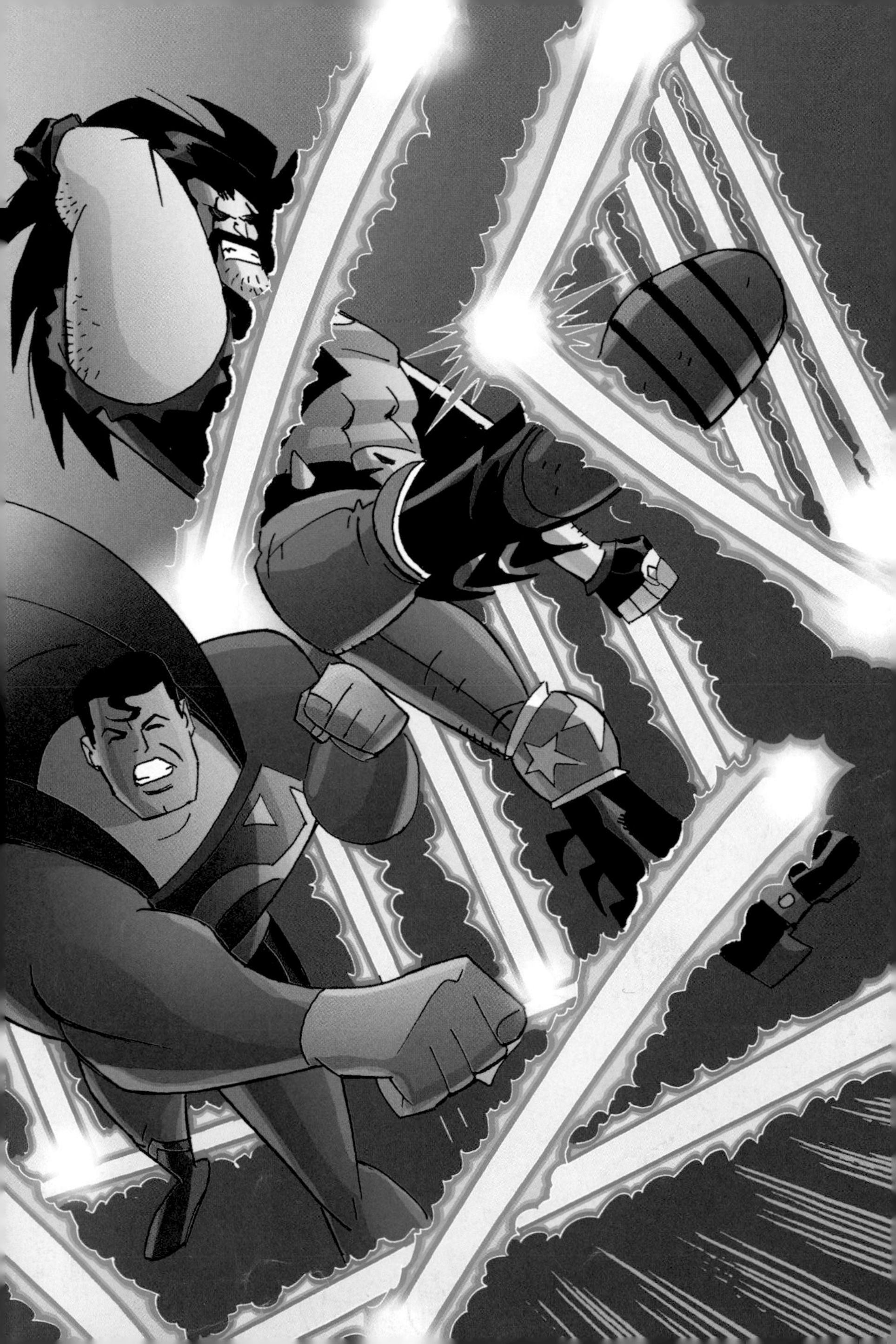

CHAPTER 5

SWEET JUSTICE

As Kalibak was sitting at the ship's controls, a loud noise startled him. **BANG!**

"What was that?" Kalibak asked.

He pointed to the rear of the ship's control room. A large dent had been made into the metal wall behind them.

"How —?" Kalibak began, but before he could finish, the sound of breaking metal interrupted him.

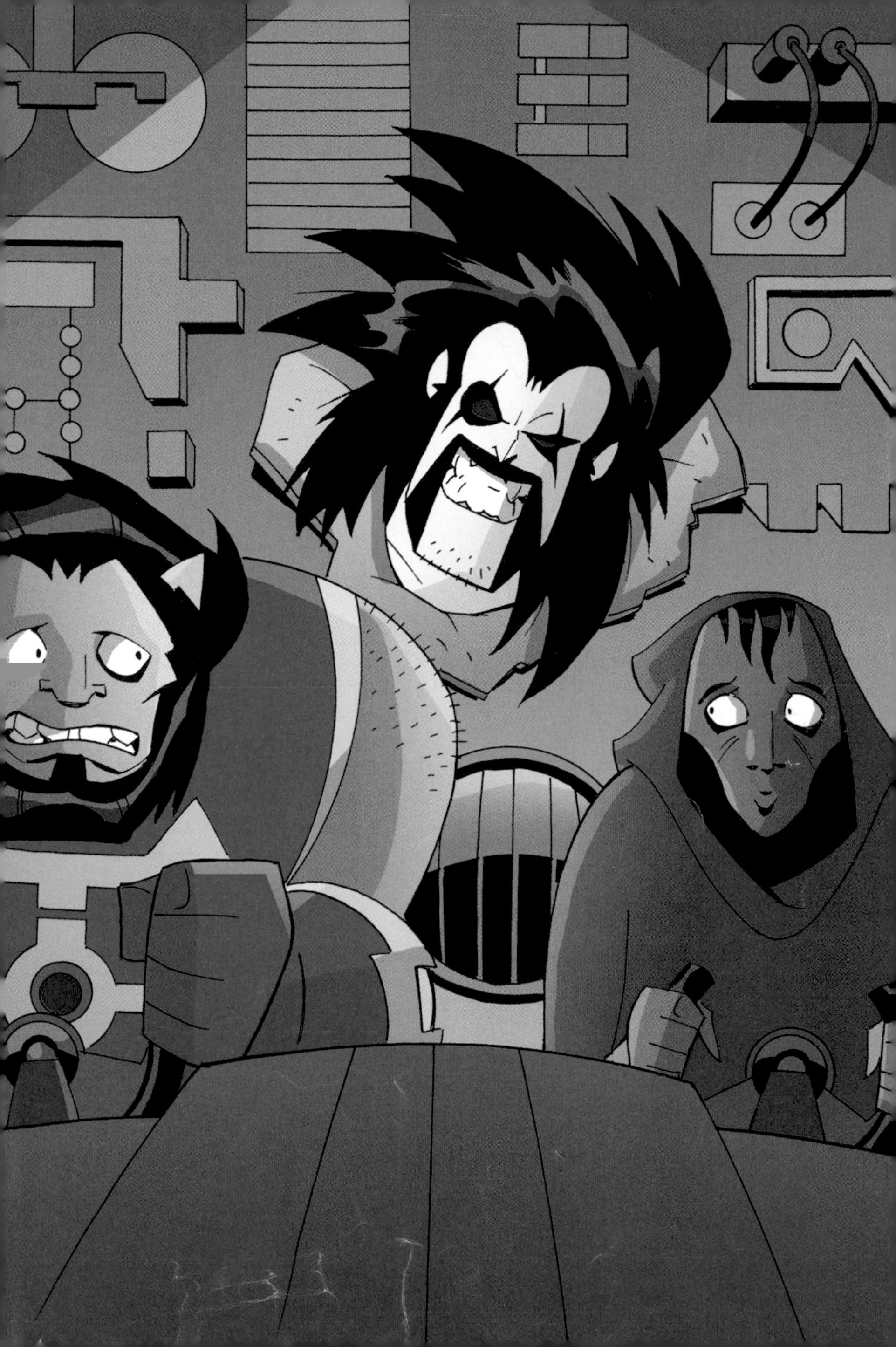

The metal wall split open, and Lobo's grinning mug poked through the gaping hole.

"You two are in for a hurtin'," Lobo said with a smile.

Kalibak and Desaad stared back at him in silent fear.

*   *   *

Much later, Lobo zoomed down toward the surface of Apokolips. He was riding his motorcycle. Kalibak and Desaad, looking bruised and battered, were tied to the back of his bike.

Instead of stopping at the landing pad, Lobo cruised toward the castle, leaving a trail of dust behind him. He drove through the castle door, down the hallway, and into the throne room.

Lobo skidded to a halt in front of Darkseid's throne.

"Where's Superman?" Darkseid asked as Lobo leaped off his bike.

"Oh, he got away," Lobo said.

"Then you won't get paid," Darkseid scowled.

"Well, I would have captured Superman," Lobo said as he pulled Kalibak and Desaad off the back of his bike and dropped them at Darkseid's feet. "Only these two goons got in my way."

"So, how about you pay me for bringing them back in one piece," Lobo demanded.

Darkseid glared disapprovingly at his son and the evil scientist. "Fine, fine," he said to Lobo, with a dismissive wave. "Take whatever you can carry."

Lobo grinned and pulled a large black sack out of his back pocket.

*   *   *

In the newsroom of the *Daily Planet*, Clark Kent typed away at his desk. Jimmy Olsen approached with a copy of that day's newspaper. On the front page was a picture of Lobo holding Lois off the ground while she kicked and screamed. The headline read "Local Reporter Battles Cosmic Biker," with the byline "by Clark Kent."

"Great photo, Jimmy," Clark said.

"Thanks, Clark," Jimmy blushed. "But, I don't get it. How did you get this story? I didn't even see you there."

"I've been working on that interview with Superman," Clark explained. "So he gave me the scoop."

"You must have a pretty good relationship with him then," Jimmy said.

"You could say that," Clark replied with a grin.

As they were talking, Perry White rushed into the room. Hot on his trail was Lois Lane.

She was waving a copy of the Daily Planet newspaper in front of him. "How could you bump my story to page two?" she demanded.

"It was an editorial choice," Mr. White replied. "Our readers like celebrity news, and you, Lois, happen to be a celebrity."

"But people were in danger. A bridge could have collapsed," Lois explained. "This is just a, just a —"

"Face it, Lois," Mr. White interrupted. "You'd rather have your story on the front page than your picture."

Mr. White stormed into his office, slamming the door shut behind him before Lois could follow.

Lois stood there dumbfounded for a second. Then she scanned the newsroom. Seeing Clark at his desk, she headed in his direction.

"You stole my scoop!" Lois scolded. "How did you get to this story first, Smallville?!"

"Well, Lois," Clark said, leaning back in his chair and smiling, "I'm afraid that's between me and the Man of Steel himself."

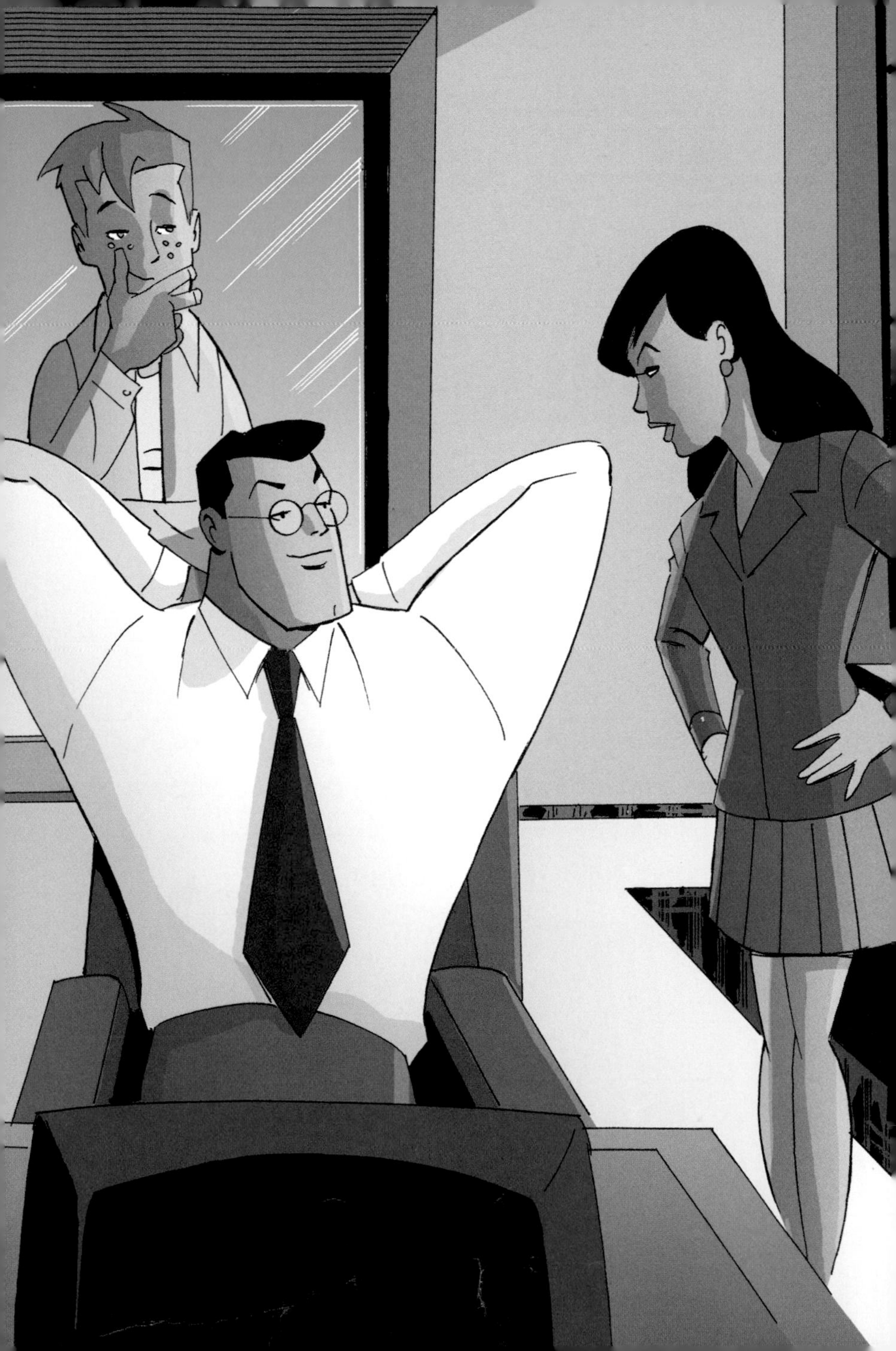

DAILY PLANET

FROM THE DESK OF CLARK KENT

WHO IS LOBO?

Lobo is known as the most successful bounty hunter in the entire universe. He always gets his man, even if it means destroying entire planets in pursuit of his prey. In fact, Lobo loves breaking things — and people — so the line of work suits him well. Despite being a self-proclaimed "bad man," Lobo is always true to his word. He will never break a promise, but he does tend to *bend* them quite often. His employers must choose their words carefully, or they'll end up in a deal they didn't quite bargain for.

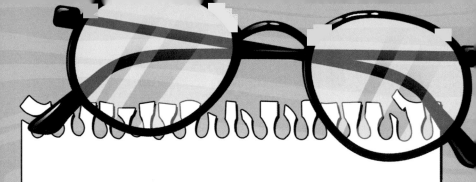

- Lobo is the last member of his race, the Czarnians, because he destroyed his own home planet in a fit of rage!

- Lobo zooms around from planet to planet atop his trusty, customized motorcycle, the Hog. Since Lobo doesn't need to breathe, he can undergo interstellar travel at super-speed without even wearing a space suit.

- Lobo's accelerated healing abilities allow him to regenerate lost limbs with great speed. In fact, Lobo can heal from any injury if he's given enough time.

- Despite his own bad body odor, Lobo has an amazing sense of smell. He is able to sniff out his prey from as far as a galaxy away! He also has the tracking skills of an expert hunter, so hiding from the Main Man is nearly impossible.

- Lobo has a variety of high-tech weaponry, including a titanium chain with a hook on its end, frag grenades, and giant carving blades. However, being the blunt instrument that he is, Lobo usually prefers to use a crowbar in combat.

BIOGRAPHIES

Blake A. Hoena earned a Masters of Fine Arts degree in Creative Writing from Minnesota State University, Mankato. Since graduating, Blake has written more than thirty books for children, including *Harley Quinn's Shocking Surprise*, *Poison Ivy's Deadly Garden*, *Under the Red Sun*, and *Livewire!*

Rick Burchett has worked as a comics artist for over 25 years. He has received the comics industry's Eisner Award three times, Spain's Haxtur Award, and he has been nominated for England's Eagle award. Rick lives with his wife and two sons near St. Louis, Missouri.

Lee Loughridge has been working in comics for more than fifteen years. He currently lives in sunny California in a tent on the beach.

GLOSSARY

conquer (KONG-kur)—to defeat and take control of something

debris (duh-BREE)—the scattered pieces of something that has been broken or destroyed

dumbfounded (DUHM-found-id)—so amazed or shocked that you cannot speak

emitted (i-MIT-id)—released or sent out something such as heat, light, or sound

inspected (in-SPEKT-id)—looked at something very carefully

menacing (MEN-uhss-ing)—dangerous

minions (MIN-yuhnz)—servants of a person in power

ruthless (ROOTH-liss)—cruel or without pity

scoop (SKOOP)—a story covered in a newspaper before anyone else reports it

winced (WINSSD)—flinched in fear of something

DISCUSSION QUESTIONS

1. Is Lobo a super-villain, a super hero, or something else? Why?

2. If you could have the powers of any character in this book, which would you choose? Discuss your answers.

3. This book has ten illustrations. Which one is your favorite? Why?

WRITING PROMPTS

1. Imagine you've just completed a very difficult bounty hunt. But, instead of gold and jewels, Darkseid has offered you anything you desire. What rewards would you choose? Write about it.

2. Write another chapter to this story. What does Lobo spend his hard-earned money on? Does Superman come after him? You decide!

3. Lobo cruises across galaxies atop his customized Hog motorcycle. Create your own space vehicle, writing about its features and cool touches. Then, draw a picture of your new ride.

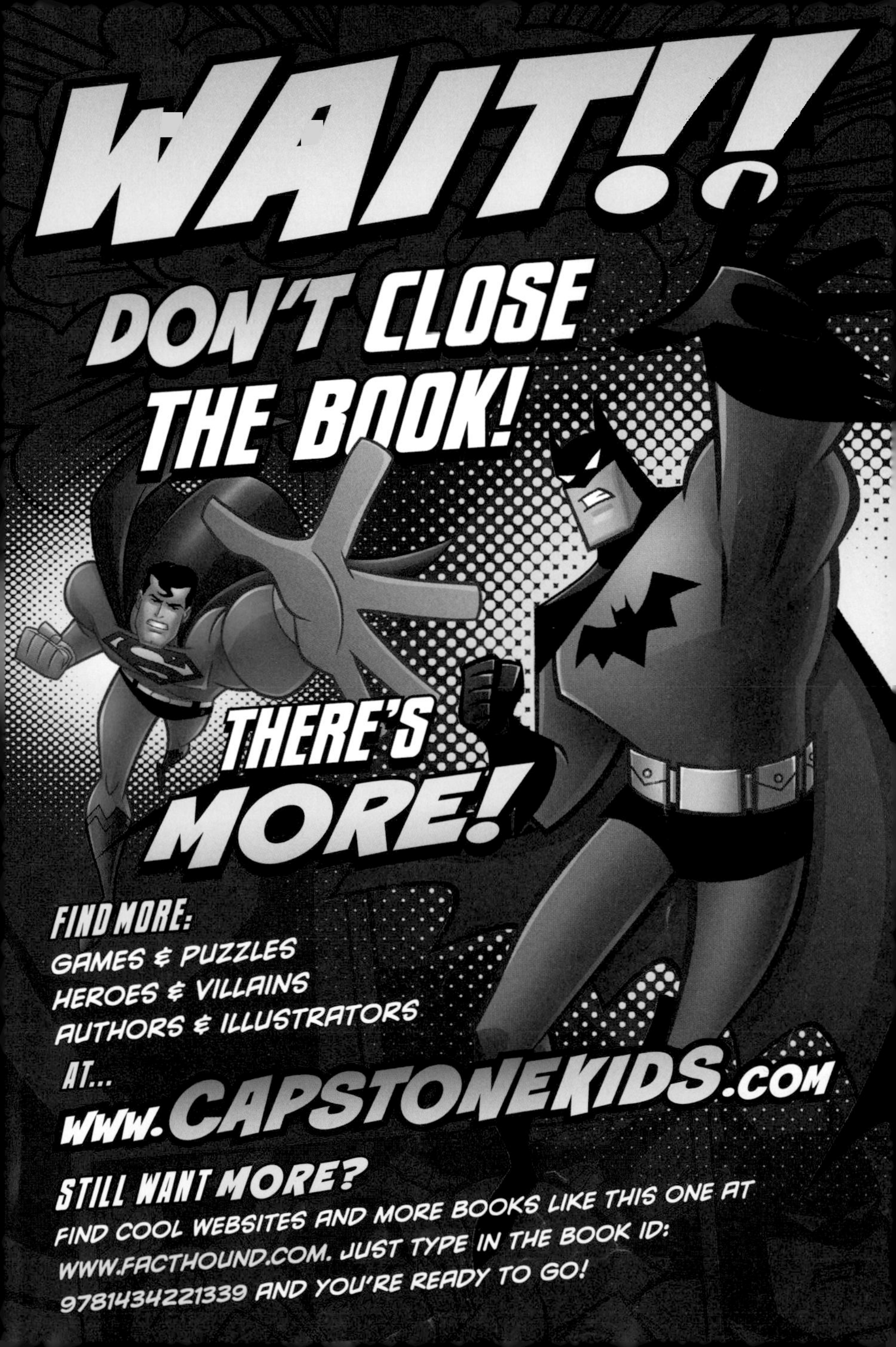
WAIT!!
DON'T CLOSE THE BOOK!
THERE'S MORE!
FIND MORE:
GAMES & PUZZLES
HEROES & VILLAINS
AUTHORS & ILLUSTRATORS
AT...
WWW.CAPSTONEKIDS.COM
STILL WANT MORE?
FIND COOL WEBSITES AND MORE BOOKS LIKE THIS ONE AT
WWW.FACTHOUND.COM. JUST TYPE IN THE BOOK ID:
9781434221339 AND YOU'RE READY TO GO!

MORE NEW
SUPERMAN
ADVENTURES!

DEEP SPACE HIJACK

PARASITE'S POWER DRAIN

PRANKSTER OF PRIME TIME

THE DEADLY DREAM MACHINE

THE SHADOW MASTERS

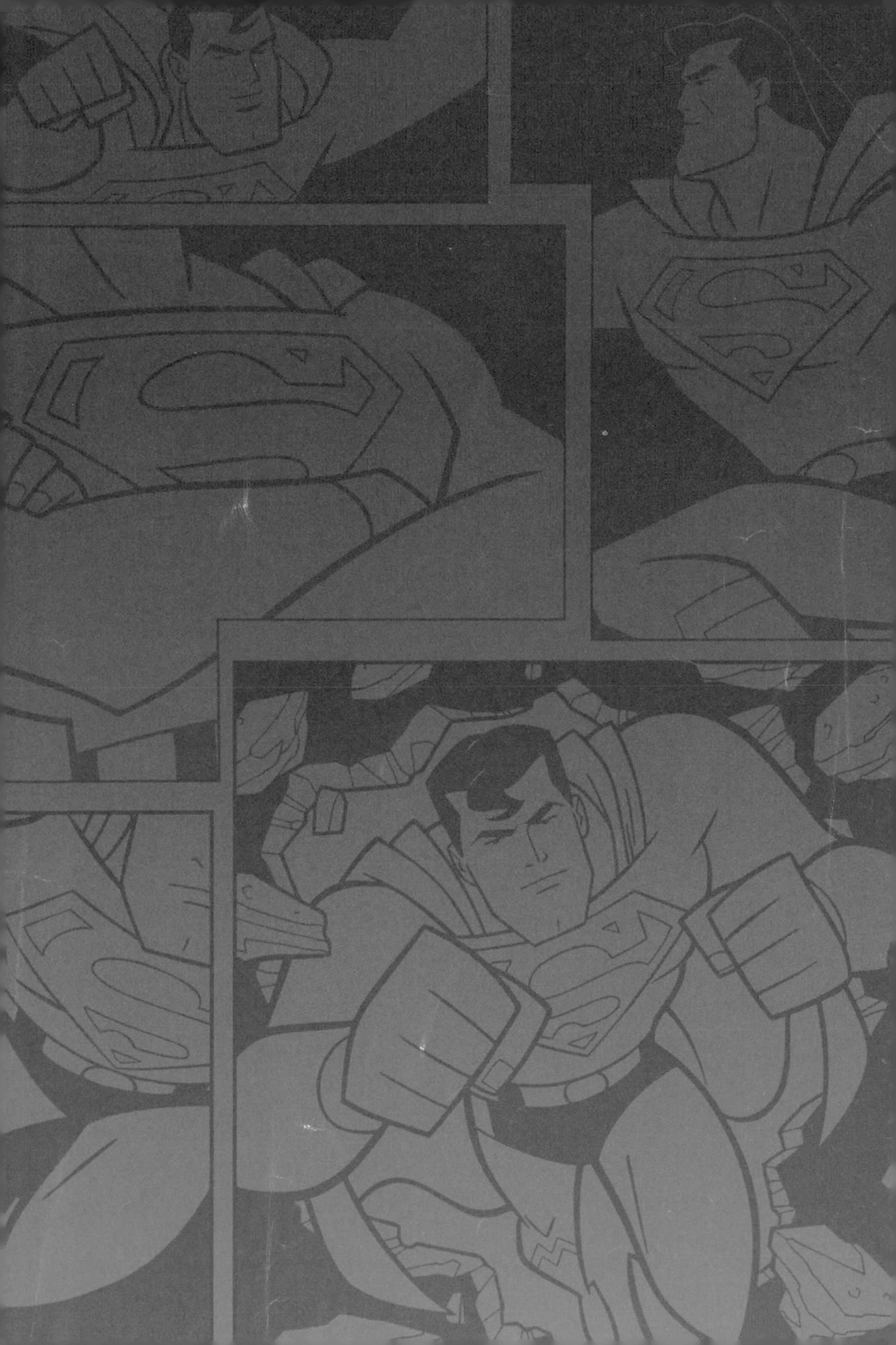

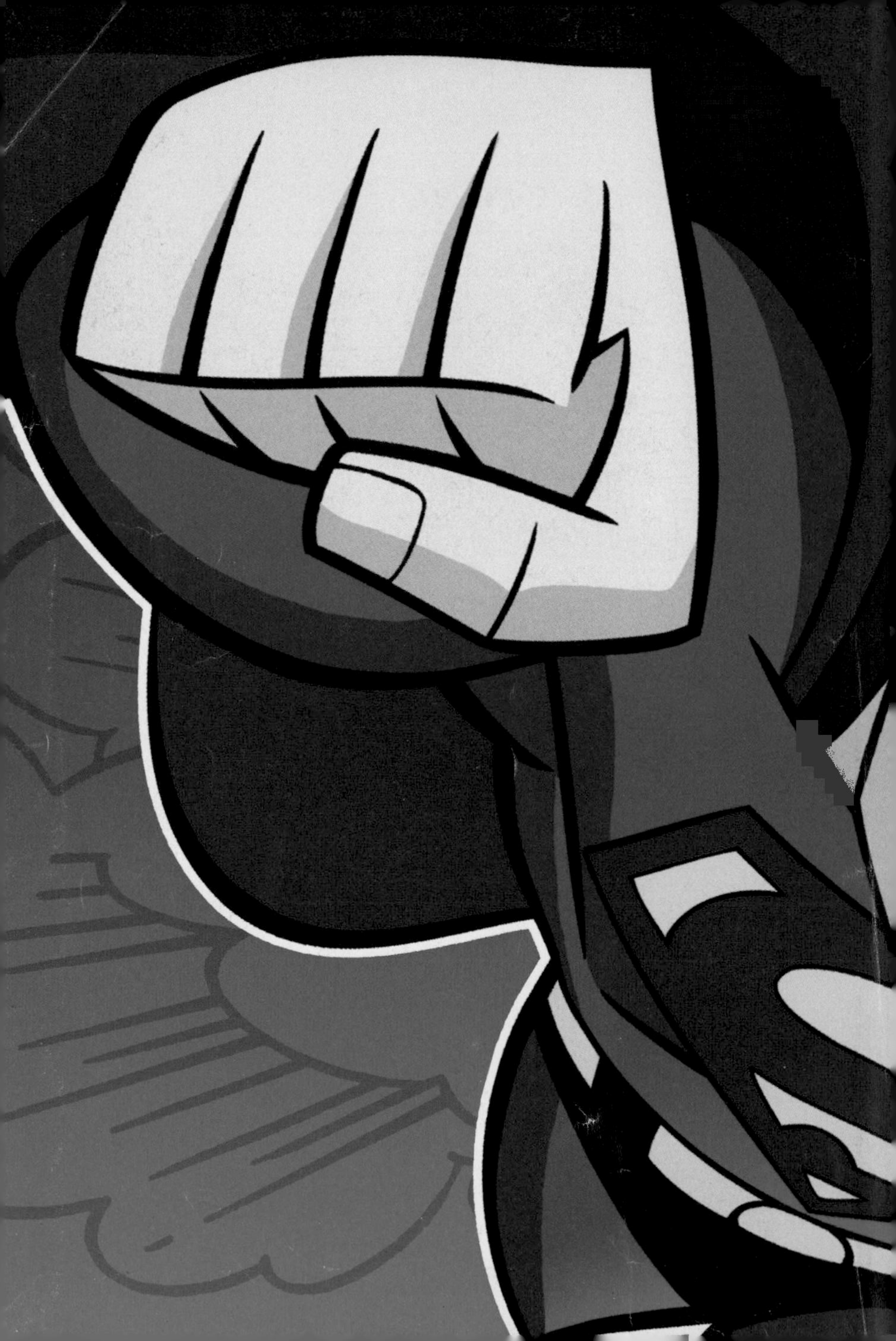